By Alyssa Gagliardi

Illustrated by Jenna Salamone

Boardwalk Fries by Alyssa Gagliardi

Copyright © 2020. All rights reserved.

ALL RIGHTS RESERVED: No part of this book may be reproduced, stored, or transmitted, in any form, without the express and prior permission in writing of Pen It! Publications, LLC. This book may not be circulated in any form of binding or cover other than that in which it is currently published.

This book is licensed for your personal enjoyment only. All rights are reserved. Pen It! Publications does not grant you rights to resell or distribute this book without prior written consent of both Pen It! Publications and the copyright owner of this book. This book must not be copied, transferred, sold or distributed in any way.

Disclaimer: Neither Pen It! Publications, or our authors will be responsible for repercussions to anyone who utilizes the subject of this book for illegal, immoral or unethical use.

This is a work of fiction. The views expressed herein do not necessarily reflect that of the publisher.

This book or part thereof may not be reproduced in any form, stored in a retrieval system, or transmitted in any form by any means-electronic, mechanical, photocopy, recording or otherwise-without prior written consent of the publisher, except as provided by United States of America copyright law.

Published by Pen It! Publications, LLC in the U.S.A.
812-371-4128   www.penitpublications.com

ISBN: 978-1-952894-02-2

Illustrated by Jenna Salamone

Ella and her brother James run up the ramp to hear the seagulls as they squawk "hello"!

Shops filled with shirts and salt-water taffy caught their eyes as they walked toward the amusement rides.

Bumper cars, log flume, tickets galore!

Ella points out the lights as they turn bright on the rollercoaster and the Ferris wheel.

Rumbling tummies crave the unforgettable taste of not popcorn by the rides, but salty, boardwalk fries!

Ella, James and the seagulls are a fan! One flies by and takes one right from Ella's hand!

Surprised she is, Ella doesn't mind sharing her yummy fries with her brother and new friend.

The End

Alyssa Gagliardi made one of her dreams a reality in 2020 when she paired up with Pen It! Publications to publish her first children's picture book!

Alyssa is a Stockton University graduate, earning a Bachelor's degree in Hospitality and Tourism Management.

Alyssa is a wife and mother of two, who loves nothing more than to spend time creating memories with her family.

CPSIA information can be obtained
at www.ICGtesting.com
Printed in the USA
LVHW072100290720
661004LV00043B/664